I0788146

MESSY BESSY

ELIZABETH KIMMINS MILLER

About the Author

Elizabeth Kimmins Miller was born and raised in NJ and lived there most of her life. She graduated from college with a bachelor's degree in Elementary Education, a master's degree in special education, and a master's degree in reading specialization. For 35 years, she has dedicated her life to the education and love of learning-disabled children and teens.

As a college professor at Centenary University, she was awarded a grant in order to start the first program of its kind in the country to help learning disabled students attend college and to be successful on the college level. The program was very successful and was duplicated in hundreds of colleges and universities across the country.

Her enduring love of children enabled her to write her first children's book. Her book is written in rhyming verse with a rhythm and story children will love.

Ms. Miller has two sons, two daughters-in-law and four grandchildren, who asked to hear her stories over and over. Ms. Miller currently lives in Middletown, Delaware with her husband.

There was a girl, her name was Bessy,
And she was very, very messy.
Her messes followed her around.
She's hard to lose, and easily found.
Her room's a mess, with piles of clothes,
But where's the floor? Just no one knows.

Can't find the chair, can't find the bed,
Bessy's buried way over her head.
She's got more stuff than anyone.
Mountains of toys that weigh a ton.
It won't be long, I have a feeling,
Bessy's mess will reach the ceiling.
There's piles of dirt all around her,
And it didn't help to yell or hound her.
It's plain to see, I must confess,
That Bessy's happy with her mess.
Dirty face and dirty hair,
Bessy didn't really care.
Piles of dirt, she left a path,
'Cause Bessy never took a bath.
And when she ate, she left a trail,
Of dirt and crumbs that all go stale.
The rotten fruit and day-old bread
smelled like something must be dead.
People begged and said, "please, Bess!"
"Somehow, you must clean up your mess!"
But Bessy never really cared,
When everyone just stopped and stared.

It got so bad, it was a worry,
She must do something in a hurry.
For Bessy's mess, it was a threat,
cause Bessy's lost her only pet.
Her puppy, Clyde, was gone for days.
Not on the pile where he always lays.
Not in her room, not in her mess,
She looked to the east and looked to the west.
He's truly gone, she really tried.
She yelled, she screamed, "oh, where is Clyde?"
In all this time, he's never strayed,
But it seemed to me, Clyde's run away.
She looked real high, and she looked low.
There's a million places Clyde could go.
And this made Bessy start to think,
Clyde ran away to avoid the stink.

He is a puppy, that's how it goes.
For Clyde developed a sensitive nose.
The more he smelled, the more he sniffed,
Clyde had no choice but to get miffed.
He was angry, he was sad,
He felt neglected and this was bad.
He ran away to save himself,
He won't come back 'til Bess gets help.
Puppies are special, you must take care.
Give lots of love, it's only fair.
The mess was too big for Clyde to climb,
His food was buried and hard to find.
He could not run, he could not play,
'Cause Bessy's mess was in the way.
His ball was gone, his favorite toy,
His bone, his bed, he got annoyed.
But the smell was really the final straw.
His sensitive nose was red and raw.
"she doesn't love me and that's a fact,
'Cause if she did, she'd clean up her act."

So he ran away, a real no-brainer.
Bess was crazy and Clyde was saner.
He must find just what he is needing,
Without the begging and the pleading.
So Bess began to realize,
Why Clyde took off with no goodbyes.
All Bess could do was wait and wait.
She feared the worst; it may be too late.
Then Bess got off her dirty couch,
And said, "no time to be a slouch.
I won't give up! There may be time,
To claim my puppy, he is still mine."
So Bessy, during all this grief,
Vowed to turn over a new leaf.

"I know! I'll call the garbage men.
They'll be here by eight, and out by ten."
"So she called, they came, and to their surprise,
They saw her mess, and couldn't believe their eyes.
"This mess is too big for guys like us.
Let's call the expert, Garbage Gus!"
So eventually, Gus did show up,
But even he said he might throw up.
"This stinks so bad, oh my poor nose.
I'll have to use our strongest hose."

So Gus cleaned and cleaned from floor to ceiling.
He cleaned the walls, which were all peeling.
And trucked away mountains of mess.
Gus hoped that this would really help Bess.
And all around, Gus did the trick.
The garbage fell just like a brick.
And even though the hose had power,
This huge clean-up went on for hours.
Gus worked his hose for days and days.
All Bess could do was pray and pray.
She really hoped that this would work,
And she was sorry for being such a jerk.

And then it happened! Her house was clean!
Her room was neat, just like a dream.
And when she walked in through the door,
She said, "I can see a shiny floor!"
"And oh my gosh! I see my bed!
And now, poor Clyde can rest his head.
I found his ball, I found his bone,
But now I wish Clyde would come home."
But first, she thanked Gus for all he did.
She couldn't do it, she was just a kid.
For Gus, it's over, it was one tough gig.
And Bessy said,"Gus, I owe you big."
 Now Bessy was hoping she could find
Her puppy Clyde and change his mind.
For surely, this was just a test,
To see if Bessy could do her best.

Then came a knock, she said, "who is it?"
Clyde came back but just to visit.
"I'm not staying," said Clyde, "it's just too messy."
"But I cleaned it up, you see?" said Bessy.
Clyde looked around. Could it be true?
The place looked clean and shiny new.
But Clyde was wary; he thought it strange.
Could messy Bessy really change?
"Yes! Yes! I can! I changed my ways.
And please, dear Clyde, I hope you stay.
I'll clean and keep this place real neat,
And take more baths so I smell sweet."
"And no more garbage and no more stink.
Here's your food, your bowl, please take a drink.
I promise,I've changed, don't make me weep,
'Cause my promises are meant to keep."

"But do you love me?" Clyde said, 'Cause that's the thing.
You've hurt me deep and it still stings.
How can I trust you to do your best?
And take good care of me without the mess?"
 "I'm just a puppy who needs a clean home,
And good food, and toys, and room to roam.
It's too hard for you Bess, you don't have the knack.
And if I leave again, I won't come back."
"Oh, please!" Said Bess, "I admit I blew it.
But I have changed and I can do it.
It's great to be clean and I am sold.
I'll prove my promise is as good as gold."
"I love you, Clyde, and I truly care.
Together we make a special pair.
Please stay and let me prove to you,
That my attitude is as good as new"

So Clyde felt better, and crawled into her lap.
He was clean, he was fed, it was time for his nap.
And Bessy was good, she earned his trust.
Between a girl and her puppy, this was a must.
You see, Clyde needed Bessy and Bessy needed Clyde.
They were missing each other and they both cried.
Now Clyde was there for Bessy to mother,
Just like one hand that washes the other.

So that's the story of Bessy and Clyde.
This is what happens if you try.
And it is not any big mystery,
Why this story went down in history.
'Cause Bessy and Clyde lived a very good life.
They stayed clean and happy with no more strife.
They played and loved with lots of laughter.
And lived happily and neatly ever after.

Dedicated to my grandchildren
for loving my stories.
I love you